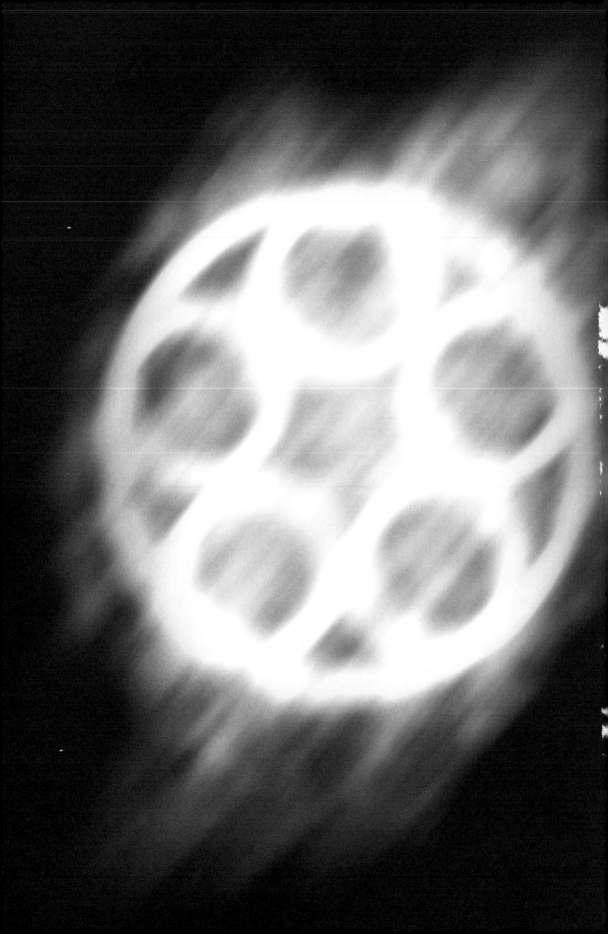

MATT FREEMAN KNOWS NOW THAT HE IS NO ORDINARY FOURTEEN YEAR OLD. HE HAS INNER POWERS – THE ABILITY TO MOVE OBJECTS OR TO WREAK HAVOC BY USING HIS MIND. BUT THESE POWERS ARE STILL LATENT, BEYOND HIS CONTROL.

THEY WERE TESTED ONCE, IN RAVEN'S GATE, WHERE MATT FOUND HIMSELF CHOSEN AS A BLOOD SACRIFICE TO OPEN A MAGIC PORTAL BETWEEN TWO DIMENSIONS. ANCIENT CREATURES OF UNIMAGINABLE EVIL, THE OLD ONES, WERE ATTEMPTING TO ENTER THE WORLD – TO DESTROY IT. AT THE VERY LAST MINUTE, MATT WAS ABLE TO STOP THEM.

BUT THE FIGHT IS NOT OVER. FIVE TEENAGERS STAND BETWEEN HUMANITY AND CHAOS. THEY ARE THE GATEKEEPERS – AND MATT IS ONE OF THEM. ONLY WHEN THEY HAVE FOUND EACH OTHER WILL THE WORLD BE SAFE.

AND A SECOND GATE IS ABOUT TO OPEN...

ANTHONY HOROWITZ

THE POWER OF FIVE: BOOK TWO

EVIL STAR

THE GRAPHIC NOVEL

adapted by TONY LEE

illustrated by
LEE O'CONNOR

WALKER

SOME PEOPLE ARE ALREADY DESCRIBING IT AS THE FIND OF A LIFETIME. IT WAS WRITTEN BY ST JOSEPH OF CORDOBA –

– A SPANISH MONK WHO TRAVELLED WITH PIZARRO TO PERU IN 1532. LATER CALLED THE 'MAD MONK OF CORDOBA', THIS DIARY MAY EXPLAIN WHY.

THE DIARY CONTAINS MANY REMARKABLE PREDICTIONS. WRITTEN FIVE HUNDRED YEARS AGO, IT DESCRIBES IN DETAIL –

– THE COMING OF MOTOR CARS, COMPUTERS AND SPACE SATELLITES. IT EVEN PREDICTS A CHURCH-CREATED FORM OF INTERNET.

THE DIARY WAS FOUND IN THE SPANISH CITY OF CORDOBA, BURIED IN THE COURTYARD OF A TENTH CENTURY MOSQUE, THE MEZQUITA.

IT'S BELIEVED TO HAVE BEEN BOUGHT AND SOLD MANY TIMES BEFORE IT WAS DISCOVERED IN A MARKET BY AN ENGLISH ANTIQUE'S DEALER, WILLIAM MORTON.

I KNEW AT ONCE WHAT IT WAS.

"*NOTHING'S* GOING TO HAPPEN TO YOU IN YORK."

SEVENTY MILES SOUTH

SCREECH

WHERE ARE YOU GOING, LOVE? A BIT LATE TO BE OUT ON YOUR OWN?

NORTH. WHERE ARE YOU HEADING?

SHEFFIELD.

THANKS FOR STOPPING – I THOUGHT I WAS GOING TO BE OUT THERE ALL NIGHT.

THIS *IS* A NICE BIG PETROL TANKER, ISN'T IT?

FULL OF LOTS AND LOTS OF USEFUL *PETROL.*

MATTHEW? ARE YOU WELL?

I... SORRY MISS. EVERYTHING'S SO STIFLING, SO HOT.

PERHAPS YOU SHOULD GO SEE MATRON.

YES, MISS.

I DON'T *BELONG* HERE. THE ONLY THING I HAVE IN COMMON IS THE UNIFORM.

IT'S TIME I *LEFT* FORREST HILL.

I FEEL BETTER ALREADY.

SHE DIDN'T KNOW WHAT SHE WAS DOING – TO STEAL A TANKER AND FIND HER WAY TO YOUR SCHOOL –

– THE **OLD ONES.** THEY INFLUENCED HER, MAYBE EVEN **FORCED** HER.

SO – YOU WANT US TO MEET THIS WILLIAM MORTON. MATT'S AGREED TO THAT. BUT IF IT MEANS PUTTING HIM IN DANGER—

THAT'S THE LAST THING ON OUR MINDS.

WE NEED MATT TO MEET WITH MORTON AT TWELVE O'CLOCK. BUT MATT IS MORE IMPORTANT THAN THE DIARY.

RIGHT NOW, IF HE'S WHO WE THINK HE IS – HE'S THE MOST **IMPORTANT** KID IN THE WORLD.

YOU'VE TOLD HIM MATT'S ONE OF THE **FIVE.** AND MORTON WANTS TO SEE IF IT'S TRUE.

HOW DOES MATT **PROVE** IT? DOES HE HAVE TO SEE INTO THE FUTURE OR BLOW SOMETHING UP?

WE DON'T KNOW. REMEMBER – HE'S READ THE DIARY. WE HAVEN'T. HE MAY KNOW MORE THAN WE DO.

ALL WE KNOW IS THAT HE'S AFRAID. AFRAID OF THE MAN HE WAS DEALING WITH IN SOUTH AMERICA.

AND HE'S AFRAID OF WHAT HE READ IN THE DIARY ITSELF. HE'S LOOKING FOR A WAY OUT.

WE DO NOT KNOW WHERE TO FIND HIM. HE CALLS US ONLY WITH HIS MOBILE PHONE.

BUT HE SAID FOR YOU TO MEET HIM AT NOON TOMORROW AT *ST. MEREDITH'S* IN MOORE STREET. ALONE.

MATT'S NOT GOING IN THERE *ALONE*!

LEAVE THAT TO ME. I HAVE ACCESS TO ALL SECURITY CAMERAS IN MOORE STREET. I'LL HAVE A *HUNDRED* OFFICERS IN THE AREA.

ONE WORD FROM ME AND THEY'LL MOVE IN.

ST. MEREDITH'S IS AN OLD CHURCH. IT MAY BE MENTIONED IN THE DIARY.

IF HE *BELIEVES* YOU - HE WILL SELL US THE DIARY. WILL YOU GO?

I WILL - IF YOU GIVE ME SOMETHING IN RETURN.

YOU *STOPPED* RICHARD BEING PUBLISHED - SO YOU CAN USE YOUR INFLUENCE TO GET HIM A JOB HERE IN LONDON.

AND I WANT TO GO TO AN *ORDINARY* SCHOOL. I WANT TO BE LEFT ALONE.

I DON'T KNOW IF WE CAN PROMISE *THAT* - YOU'RE PART OF THIS.

BUT IF THERE'S ANY WAY WE CAN LEAVE YOU OUT OF IT, WE WILL.

MATT — WE WANT TO SEND YOU TO PERU.

IT WASN'T YOUR FAULT, BUT WE'VE LOST THE DIARY AND IT'S A CATASTROPHE. WHOEVER WAS BIDDING FOR IT IN SOUTH AMERICA HAS IT — OR *WILL* HAVE IT SOON.

THE DIARY WILL SHOW THEM HOW TO FIND, AND POSSIBLY *OPEN* A GATE.

THERE'S NOTHING MATT CAN DO. YOU'RE SENDING HIM HALFWAY AROUND THE *WORLD* — WHAT'S THE POINT?

THINK OF IT LIKE CHESS. MORTON DIED — WE LOST A PAWN. BY SENDING MATT, WE ADVANCE A KNIGHT.

WE MAY BE TOO LATE. IT MAY NOT HELP. BUT AT LEAST IT SHOWS WE ARE STILL ON THE ATTACK.

THE BOY AND THE GATE ARE LINKED. WHATEVER HAPPENS IN PERU — HE SHOULD *BE* THERE.

WE HAVE ONE LEAD. MORTON'S PHONE WAS WITH THE BODY. ON IT WERE THREE CALLS TO A NUMBER IN LIMA, PERU.

SALAMANDA NEWS INTERNATIONAL.

ONE OF THE BIGGEST BUSINESSES IN THE WHOLE DAMNED CONTINENT. AND ITS FRONTMAN, DIEGO SALAMANDA — IS THE *RICHEST* MAN IN PERU.

HE MAY HAVE BEEN THE ONE BUYING THE DIARY. IF HE IS, THAT'S BAD NEWS. HE'S POWERFUL.

THANK YOU FOR SEEING ME, NATHALIE. I DIDN'T KNOW WHO ELSE TO COME TO.

THERE'S NO NEED TO THANK ME, SUSAN. IN MY ELEVEN YEARS WITH THE NEXUS, MY DOOR'S ALWAYS BEEN OPEN TO YOU.

MATTHEW FREEMAN IS STILL LOST, BUT IT'S NOW CONFIRMED THERE WAS A *GUNFIGHT* NEAR JORGE CHAVEZ AIRPORT.

RICHARD COLE WAS KIDNAPPED – BUT MATTHEW MANAGED TO GET AWAY.

AS FAR AS WE KNOW, HE HASN'T BEEN SEEN SINCE.

WE SENT HIM TO PERU BECAUSE WE WANTED SOMETHING TO HAPPEN.

I WAS HOPING YOU COULD HELP. YOU HAVE BUSINESS DEALINGS IN SOUTH AMERICA...

BUT WE MUST BE CAREFUL. SALAMANDA IS OUR NUMBER ONE SUSPECT.

IT SEEMS WE GOT MORE THAN WE *BARGAINED* FOR. WHAT SHALL WE DO?

I COULD TALK TO DIEGO SALAMANDA IF YOU LIKE?

I'VE NEVER MET HIM, BUT WE'VE SPOKEN MANY TIMES ON THE TELEPHONE.

IT SEEMS MORE THAN LIKELY THAT *HE'S* THE ONE TRYING TO OPEN THE GATE.

I DO NOT CARE WHAT IS A POSSIBILITY AND WHAT IS NOT – I GIVE YOU THE INSTRUCTIONS AND YOU WILL *OBEY.*

– IT'S CAPTAIN RODRIGUEZ!

THE SILVER SWAN MUST BE EN LA POSICION – AH, IN *POSITION* FIVE DAYS FROM NOW AT MIDNIGHT EXACTLY.

YOU WILL HAVE THE RESPONSIBILITY FOR THIS. DO YOU UNDERSTAND, MISS KLEIN?

IT WILL BE DONE. BUT I AM NEEDING SOON THE ... I MUST HAVE THE *COORDINATES.*

YOU WILL HAVE THE COORDINATES AS SOON AS I HAVE THEM MYSELF.

MY AGENTS HAVE BEEN TO THE NAZCA DESERT BUT HAVE STILL *FAILED* TO FIND THE PLATFORM. THE DIARY GAVE ME AN APPROXIMATE POSITION BUT I PREFER TO LEAVE NOTHING TO CHANCE.

GUARDS!

I NEED TO USE A PHONE.

I'M SORRY - WE DON'T ALLOW NON PAYING—

I AM PAYING. HERE YOU GO.

NOW, WHERE'S THE PHONE?

- CLICK -

MATTHEW? IS THAT YOU?

MISTER FABIAN?

WHERE ARE YOU? HOW ARE YOU? ARE YOU ALL RIGHT?

YEAH - I'M FINE.

WE'VE ALL BEEN SO WORRIED ABOUT YOU! I NEARLY WENT CRAZY WHEN YOU AND RICHARD DIDN'T SHOW UP IN LIMA AND ALBERTO TOLD ME WHAT HAPPENED!

IS RICHARD WITH YOU?

NO - HE'S NOT.

I'M OK - BUT I NEED YOUR HELP.

OF COURSE. YOU DON'T NEED TO WORRY ABOUT ANYTHING NOW.

JUST TELL ME WHERE YOU ARE AND HOW I CAN REACH YOU.

I'M IN CUZCO. IT'S A LONG STORY.

THEN TELL ME. AND AS SOON AS I PUT THIS PHONE DOWN -

- I'M ON MY WAY.

AS A MATTER OF FACT, I HAVE A PRETTY GOOD IDEA. LET'S HAVE SOME TEA BEFORE WE COVER THIS BACK UP.

AND WHILE WE'RE SITTING DOWN, WE CAN HAVE A TALK.

I'VE TOLD YOU ABOUT THE *MYSTERY* OF THE NAZCA LINES.

NOW I'VE GOT TO EXPLAIN MY *SOLUTION* TO THE MYSTERY.

I'VE STUDIED THE LINES FOR MOST OF MY LIFE. TO ME THEY WERE PERFECT.

BUT AS THE YEARS WENT ON, I REALIZED I WAS *WRONG*. THAT THERE WAS SOMETHING *EVIL* ABOUT THEM.

"THE PICTURES ARE BEAUTIFUL BUT – TO THE NAZCAN PEOPLE TWO THOUSAND YEARS AGO – THEY WERE *TERRIFYING*."

"EVEN THE MONKEY, REACHING OUT WITH ITS SPINDLY ARMS. IT HAS *FOUR* FINGERS ON EACH HAND..."

WHY DO YOU THINK THE PEOPLE WHO DREW THE LINES GAVE IT ONE FINGER TOO *FEW*?

MAYBE THEY COULDN'T COUNT.

NO – THEY COULD COUNT PERFECTLY WELL.

IN THEIR SOCIETY, DEFORMITY IS SOMETHING TO BE *FEARED*, A BAD OMEN.

ONE WEEK LATER

RADIESTHESIA.

IT'S ONE OF MANY NAMES WE HAVE FOR *FAITH HEALING.* THE LAYING ON OF HANDS.

AND PEDRO?

WELL, THE INCAS SEEM TO THINK HE WAS ONE OF THEIR OWN, SO IT'S NO SURPRISE THAT HE CAN DO IT.

HE SAVED MATT'S LIFE. THAT'S ALL WE NEED TO KNOW.

YOU OK? YOU'VE BEEN VERY QUIET RECENTLY – NOT YOUR *OLD* SELF.

IT'S THIS PAPER THAT MISS ASHWOOD SENT ME. THE ARTICLE THAT SHE HIGHLIGHTED. LOOK.

CHURCH DISPUTES DISAPPEARING BOY?

AN ABBEY OUTSIDE LUCCA IN SAN GALGANO CLAIMS THEY ENCOUNTERED A BOY WHO SPOKE ENGLISH, PICKED A FLOWER AND THEN *DISAPPEARED!*

THE DOOR THAT HE CAME THROUGH WAS NOT ONLY LOCKED – BUT BRICKED UP *HUNDREDS OF YEARS* AGO!

THE DOOR HAS A CURSE ON IT – THE APPEARANCE OF THE BOY SIGNALS THE BEGINNING OF THE *LAST JUDGEMENT.*

THIS WAS *YOU!* AND THAT DOOR IN LONDON!

WE HAVE TO TALK ABOUT WHAT HAPPENED.

THE INCAS TOLD ME THE GATE WOULD OPEN AND THE OLD ONES WOULD COME INTO THE WORLD.

AND THEY WERE *RIGHT.* SALAMANDA KNEW IT TOO. I SUPPOSE IT WAS IN THE DIARY.

WHERE IS THE DIARY?

SALAMANDA HAD IT. NOW HE'S DEAD, WE'LL NEVER KNOW.

I THOUGHT PEDRO AND I COULD STOP THE GATE FROM OPENING, BUT I SEE NOW THAT SOME THINGS *CAN'T* BE CHANGED. THEY HAPPENED AS THEY'RE *SUPPOSED* TO.

WE *WON* THE FIRST TIME – IN ENGLAND. WE MANAGED TO CLOSE RAVEN'S GATE.

BUT THIS TIME – WE *LOST.*

NO...

YES. I'M SORRY, BUT IT'S THE TRUTH. I SAW THE OLD ONES. AND I DIDN'T HAVE THE *STRENGTH* TO FIGHT THEM, EVEN WITH PEDRO.

THEY ARE HERE, IN THE WORLD. I WOUNDED THEM. PERHAPS THEY ARE *RESTING,* WAITING UNTIL THEY REGAIN THEIR STRENGTH.

I CAN FEEL THEM. THERE'S A COLDNESS IN THE AIR. THEY'RE SPREADING OUT, MAKING THEIR PLANS. AND SOON IT WILL *BEGIN.*

THERE ARE *FIVE* OF US. FOUR BOYS AND A GIRL. WE'RE ALL THE SAME AGE AND WE'VE ALL BEEN BORN FOR THE SAME REASON.

END OF BOOK TWO

ANTHONY HOROWITZ is the author of the number one
bestselling Alex Rider books and The Power of Five series.
He has enjoyed huge success as a writer for both children and adults,
most recently with his highly acclaimed Sherlock Holmes novel,
The House of Silk.

He has won numerous awards, including the Bookseller/Nielsen Author
of the Year Award, The Children's Book of the Year Award at the
British Book Awards, and the Red House Children's Book Award.
Anthony has also created and written many major television series,
including *Injustice, Collision* and the award-winning *Foyle's War.*

You can find out more about Anthony and his books at:
www.anthonyhorowitz.com
www.alexrider.com
www.powerof5.co.uk

TONY LEE is a New York Times number one bestselling author of graphic novels. His titles include *Pride and Prejudice and Zombies*, *Superboy*, *Spider Man* and *Doctor Who*. *Hope Falls* and *Harker* are both being developed into feature films. *Danger Academy* is being developed into a US television show. In 2012 Tony's *Doctor Who* comic won the Eagle Award for Favourite Single Story. *Outlaw: The legend of Robin Hood* and *Excalibur: The Legend of King Arthur* have both been shortlisted for the Young Adult Library Services Association's Books For Teens award and the next title in this highly acclaimed Heroes and Heroines series is *Messenger: The Legend of Joan of Arc*, illustrated by Sam Hart and published by Walker Books. Outside of comics Tony writes audio plays, film and TV scripts and lectures across the UK on reluctant reading in his Change the Channel talk.

www.tonylee.co.uk

LEE O'CONNOR is a British comics artist and illustrator whose work has appeared in the first Power of Five graphic novel *Raven's Gate* – also published by Walker Books – the cult European comics magazine *Heavy Metal*, the *Phonogram* series from Image Comics, the *Iraq* graphic novel, published by the international humanitarian charity War on Want, numerous anthologies, small-press and indie comics on both sides of the Atlantic, magazines, book covers and storyboards for film and music video. He has lectured on illustration in Australia and painted murals in New Zealand.

Currently he is developing comics with the celebrated Mancunian author Jeff Noon.

Lee lives in the wilds of rural Devon, next to an Iron Age hill fort.

www.leeoconnor.com

This is a work of fiction. Names, characters, places
and incidents are either the product of the author's
imagination or, if real, are used fictitiously. All statements,
activities, stunts, descriptions, information and material
of any other kind contained herein are included for
entertainment purposes only and should not be relied on
for accuracy or replicated as they may result in injury.

First published 2014 by Walker Books Ltd
87 Vauxhall Walk, London SE11 5HJ

10 9 8 7 6 5 4 3 2 1

Text and illustrations © 2014 Walker Books Ltd

Based on the original novel *Evil Star*
© 1985, 2006 Stormbreaker Productions Ltd
Power of 5 logo ™ © 2010 Walker Books Ltd

Anthony Horowitz has asserted his moral rights.

This book has been typeset in CC Dave Gibbons

Printed and bound in Singapore

British Library Cataloguing in Publication Data:
a catalogue record for this book is available from the
British Library

ISBN 978-1-4063-1130-3

www.walker.co.uk

www.powerof5.co.uk